KU-054-343

£3.99

rainbow

ANNUAL 1990

Contents

Words by Clive Hopwood

Copyright © 1989 by
Thames Television Limited.
All rights reserved.
Published in Great Britain by
World International Publishing Limited,
An Egmont Company,
Egmont House, P.O. Box 111, Great Ducie Street,
Manchester M60 3BL.
Printed in Italy.
ISBN 7235 6850 2

A DAY IN THE COUNTRY

It is the summer holidays. Geoffrey, George, Bungle and Zippy decide to have a special day out.

"Where shall we go?" asks Geoffrey.

George, Bungle and Zippy have a think. "We would like to go out in the country," says George.

"It's such a lovely day," says Bungle. "It seems such a pity to stay here. We could go and explore in the country."

"Oh yes!" says Zippy. "Can we go, Geoffrey, please?"

Geoffrey would like to go to the country as well. "We can go on the bus," he says. "It stops at the end of our road. If we stay on until the end of its journey we shall be in the countryside."

"Oh good!" cry Zippy, George and Bungle. They rush to put on their shoes.

"Wait a minute," says Geoffrey. "It takes a little while to get to the country. It's more sensible to go for the whole day. It makes the journey more worthwhile."

"Oh good!" cry Zippy, George and Bungle. Once

more they run to put on their shoes.

"Wait a minute," says Geoffrey again. "If we are going out into the country for the day we will need to take something to eat and drink."

"Oh yes, of course," says George.

"You are clever, Geoffrey," says Bungle. "You think of everything."

"That's a good idea," says Zippy. "I don't want to be hungry. I want to take lots of lovely things to eat and drink."

"What shall we take?" asks Geoffrey.

"I like baked beans," says Zippy quickly. (Baked beans are his favourite food this week.)

Geoffrey laughs. "Baked beans are no good to take on a day out," he says. "They need to be heated up. And we would need a pan to cook them in."

George nods. "I agree. The cooker is much too big to take with us on the bus. We need to think of things we don't need to cook."

"I know," says Bungle. "We can take some sandwiches. We can have a picnic!"

"Oh yes!" says Zippy. "That's a good idea. I want cheese sandwiches."

"I'd like some salad sandwiches," says George. "With salad cream on."

"What kind of sandwiches do you like, Bungle?" asks Geoffrey.

Bungle thinks for a moment. "I like cheese. And I like salad . . . I know," he says, "we can make some egg sandwiches as well."

They have a look in the cupboards to see if they have everything. Together they butter the bread and make the sandwiches. They wrap different ones in different bags.

"What else can we take?" asks Geoffrey.

"We can take some fruit," says George. "Apples, oranges and bananas."

"Can we have some crisps as well?" asks Zippy. "I like crisps."

"What about something to drink?" asks Bungle. "Can we take some orange squash?"

Soon they are all ready.

Geoffrey packs a bag. In it there are the sandwiches, crisps, fruit and a bottle of orange squash. Geoffrey puts in some biscuits too.

They walk along the road to the bus stop. Soon the bus comes along. Geoffrey pays for the tickets.

They all sit and look out of the window as the bus goes along. At last they arrive.

"Is this the country?" asks George.

"Yes," says the bus conductor. "This is where the bus stops. Now the driver is going to turn it round and drive back to town."

"Are you coming to pick us up later?" asks Bungle.

"Oh yes," says the bus conductor. "The bus comes back here every hour."

"Oh good," says Zippy. "See you later."

The bus drives away. Geoffrey, George, Zippy and Bungle walk down the road. Soon they come to a bridge. Bungle carefully looks over it.

"It's a river, Geoffrey," he says. "Can we have our picnic here?"

They climb down to the riverbank.

"Listen," says George. "You can hear the sound of the water." They listen. It gurgles and burbles and bubbles.

"Stay well away from the edge," says Geoffrey. "We don't want you falling in."

"There's a fish!" says Bungle. But it is only a piece of wood floating in the water.

"Look, there's a bird in the tree," says Zippy.

"Sssh!" says George. "Be quiet." He points up the hill. "There's a rabbit!" he says quietly, but very excited.

They unpack their picnic. They eat the sandwiches and the crisps. They drink the orange squash and have a biscuit. Then they eat the fruit.

After they have eaten they have a game with a ball. Then they go exploring in the woods with Geoffrey. They find wild flowers. They see butterflies. They hear the birds sing. They hear small animals rustling in the bushes. They have a lovely time.

At last it is time to go. The sun is going down. They pack up all the things. Geoffrey makes sure they leave no rubbish behind.

The bus is waiting at the bus stop. They climb aboard.

"I don't want to go home," says George sadly.

"It's lovely in the country," agrees Bungle.

"Can we come again?" asks Zippy.

"Of course," says Geoffrey. "We can come for a day out in the countryside another day."

"Hurray!" cry Zippy, George and Bungle as the bus drives them home.

PLANTS AND ANIMALS

There are many plants and animals that grow and live in the countryside. How many do you know?

There are lots of wild animals who live in the country. Some you do not see very often because they stay out of sight . . . but others you can see if you keep quiet and watch.

The Owl

You don't often see an owl, but you can tell an owl when you hear one. They sing "too-wit too-woo". Owls come out at night time. They build their homes in the trees. Sometimes they live in farmers' barns.

The Fieldmouse

Fieldmice build their nests above the ground. Each summer they gather up lots of grains of corn and store them. In the winter they have a long sleep. They feed from their store when they wake up.

The Rabbit

Rabbits live in holes under the ground. Their homes are called warrens. Rabbits have long ears and fluffy tails.

Trees

There are all kinds of different trees. They all have different shaped leaves. Some trees drop their leaves in autumn. Other trees keep their leaves all the year round.

Flowers

Hundreds of wild flowers grow in the country. They are every colour you can think of. Don't pick wild flowers – if they are lovely to look at, leave them for other people to enjoy.

Wheat

Farmers grow things to eat in their fields. Some things they grow for us to eat. Other things they grow for their animals to eat. Wheat is golden yellow when it is ready to pick. We make bread, cereals and biscuits from it.

11

Cows

Farmers keep cows for their milk. A lot of cows together are called a herd. The farmer keeps cows in fields. They eat grass.

Each day the farmer milks the cows. Then the milk is put into bottles. We also make butter, cream and cheese from milk. Cows go "moo".

Sheep

Some farmers keep sheep. Sheep eat grass. It helps to make their woolly coats grow. Every year the farmer shears the sheep. The wool is used to make clothes and other things. If you go into the country in the spring you may see some baby lambs. Sheep go "baa".

Bees

There are many insects in the country. If you are quiet you can hear them humming and buzzing about. Bees collect nectar from the flowers. They use it to make honey.

Butterflies

There are all sorts of different butterflies. They come in many different colours. They begin life as little caterpillars. As they grow older they grow wings and become beautiful butterflies.

Chickens

Chickens lay eggs. If a lot of chickens are together they make a big noise. They all go "cluck-cluck" very loudly. They lay their eggs and the farmer collects them in baskets to send them to the shops.

Remember, say Bungle, George and Zippy . . . When you are in the countryside be kind and thoughtful to the plants and animals. The countryside is their home.

Never leave any litter behind.
Always shut any gates after you.
Don't pick wild flowers.
Don't let your dog frighten the animals.

A NATURE DIARY

Bungle, George and Zippy enjoy going to the countryside. But there are lots of plants and animals that grow and live in towns too.

Wild flowers grow by the roadside and often in people's gardens. There are birds to see and hear. Butterflies and bees and other insects will visit your garden. If you leave a saucer of milk out you may attract a hedgehog.

Look out for plants and animals where you live. Bungle, George and Zippy keep a Nature Diary. When they see a new plant or animal they put it in their diary. Perhaps you would like to keep one as well.

"We use an exercise book," says Bungle.

"When we see a plant or animal," says George, "we write it down in our Nature Diary."

"We draw pictures of them too," says Zippy. "And colour them in."

"Sometimes," says Bungle, "we find a picture in a magazine. We cut it out and stick it in our Nature Diary."

Today there is a
butterfly in our garden.

A hedgehog comes to our garden.
We feed it bread and milk.
Sometimes she brings
her babies.

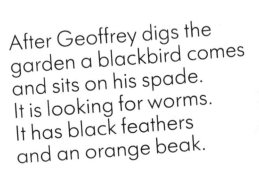

After Geoffrey digs the
garden a blackbird comes
and sits on his spade.
It is looking for worms.
It has black feathers
and an orange beak.

15

ON THE MOVE

Geoffrey is taking Bungle, George and Zippy to the playground. They like the playground.

There are swings with bright yellow seats. There is also a roundabout.

In the corner by the sand pit there is a slide. You climb the ladder to the top and slide down to the bottom.

Bungle, George and Zippy always have a good time in the playground. There are lots of things to play on.

"I want to go on the swings first," says Bungle. He goes over and sits on a swing. "Watch me," he says.

Zippy wants to go on the swings too.

"Watch me," says Zippy.

Bungle is swinging backwards and forwards. Zippy starts to swing as well.

"Do you want to go on a swing, George?" asks Geoffrey.

George is not sure. "I don't know, Geoffrey," he says.

"Are you a little bit afraid?" asks Geoffrey.

George looks at Geoffrey. "Yes," he says, "I am."

Geoffrey holds George's hand. "If you want a go, George," he says, "I'll go with you. It's quite safe."

They walk towards the swings. "I don't want to go high," says George.

"No, George," promises Geoffrey. "Not high."

"And, Geoffrey," George says.

"Yes, George," Geoffrey says.

"I don't want to go fast," says George.

"No, George," Geoffrey says. "Not fast. Not high. Let's try that small swing."

"Look at me, Geoffrey!" says Bungle.

"No, look at me, Geoffrey!" says Zippy. Zippy turns to look at Bungle. "I'm going higher than you, Bungle."

"No you're not," says Bungle.

"Yes, I am," says Zippy. "Look." He makes the swing go a little higher.

"That's not fair," says Bungle. "You're cheating. Anyway, I'm going faster than you. Look, Geoffrey. Look at me."

"No, look at me, Geoffrey," says Zippy.

"Will you two stop it?" says Geoffrey firmly. "Don't be so silly. And I've told you before, Zippy and Bungle. Don't try to swing too high or too fast. It is not safe."

"Oh, Geoffrey," says Zippy. "I'm not going really fast."

"Yes, you are," says Bungle.

"Be quiet, both of you," says Geoffrey. "We're here to enjoy ourselves. We're not here to argue. Be nice to one another. Have fun."

"Sorry, Geoffrey," say Zippy and Bungle.

Geoffrey tells them to say sorry to each other. They do. Everyone is friends again.

Geoffrey helps George to sit on the seat of the swing. It has a back to lean on and arms to hold on to.

Geoffrey holds the swing steady.

"Isn't it funny," says George.

"What is?" asks Geoffrey.

"It's just like a chair with no legs," says George. "How can I sit on a chair with no legs?"

Geoffrey laughs. "It's all right, George. A swing doesn't have legs. It doesn't need them."

Geoffrey points to the chains. "See. The chains hold it up."

George sits on the swing. Geoffrey gives it a gentle push. George first swings forwards and then he swings backwards. Forwards and backwards. To and fro. "Do you like it, George?" asks Geoffrey.

"Ooh yes," says George. "It's lovely."

Bungle stops his swing and

gets off. "I am going on the roundabout now," he says.

"Me too," says Zippy. He jumps off his swing and falls over. "Ow!" he says. "My arm hurts!"

"You are silly, Zippy," says Bungle. "Wait for the swing to stop first."

"Bungle's right," says Geoffrey. "You must all promise to be careful."

"We promise, Geoffrey," say Zippy, George and Bungle.

"Are you okay, Zippy?" asks Geoffrey.

Zippy rubs his arm. "Yes," he says. "I won't do that again, Geoffrey."

"Come on, Zippy," says Bungle. "Let's go on the roundabout."

"No," Zippy says. "I want to go on the slide."

Bungle runs over to the roundabout. Holding on tightly he walks around the roundabout giving it a little push. Then he sits on.

Zippy climbs the steps of the slide. He holds on to the rail on each side. At the top he sits down carefully. Then he slides down to the bottom.

"Whoosh!" says Zippy, as he slides down.

"Wheee!" says Bungle, as he spins round.

"Zoom!" says George as he swings to and fro.

Zippy has another go on the slide. George says he wants a go on the roundabout. It is his favourite.

First, Geoffrey stops the roundabout. "You must always stop the roundabout before you get on," says George. "Geoffrey says so."

"I know," says Bungle. "Get on, George. Geoffrey is going to give us a ride."

"Wait for me!" says Zippy.

Geoffrey waits. Zippy climbs on.

"All aboard!" cries Bungle.

"Whoo-whoo!" George says.

Geoffrey begins to push the roundabout. Round it goes, slowly at first, then a little faster. George, Zippy and Bungle hold on tightly. They like it so much they ask Geoffrey to keep pushing them for a long ride.

Then it is time to go home for tea.

"Geoffrey," says George, "don't you want a go on anything?"

Geoffrey looks a bit tired. "No thanks, George," he says. "I think I'll go home and have a lie down instead."

"You should join in more," says Bungle. "It's good for you."

"Yes," says Zippy. "We can come again tomorrow, can't we, Geoffrey?"

Geoffrey smiles. "We'll see," he says. "We'll see."

LET'S GO!

Bungle, George and Zippy all like things that go. When they are in the playground they go on the rides. Half the fun of the rides is the pretending part.

What does Bungle pretend when he's on the roundabout? Where does Zippy pretend he is when he's on the slide? And what does George pretend he's doing when he's on the swing?

Bungle is on the roundabout. "Wheee!" He goes round and round. "It's like being on a train," he says. "Whoo-whoo!"

Zippy is on the slide. "Whoosh!" He slides all the way from the top to the bottom. "It's like being in a boat," he says, "riding down a river. Sploosh!"

George is on the swing. "Zoom!" He swings backwards and forwards, to and fro. "It's like flying in an aeroplane," he says. "Zow!"

THE DOLL WHO FORGOT HOW TO DANCE

The jumble sale was over. The hall was empty except for a stack of boxes. They were full of left over jumble. Two men came in. One was young, and the other was an older man. They began to load the boxes into a van.

A few minutes later they drove up to a house. The two men unloaded the boxes. Soon everything was neatly stacked in the garage. The door was closed.

It was very quiet in the garage. The light was dim, and there was a chill, musty smell.

Presently a small sound could be heard. It was coming from one of the boxes on top. Slowly the lid began to open.

A pair of furry ears appeared, then a little furry face. It was a toy rabbit: "Am I glad to get out of there," he said. One of his ears was rather torn, he only had one eye, and his fur was rather dirty and scruffy.

A sailor climbed up beside him. He was made of wood. His paint was very chipped and patchy.

"What about me?" said a tiny voice from the bottom of the box. The rabbit reached down and picked up a small clockwork mouse. Her clockwork motor didn't work any more.

"Nobody wanted to buy me," said the clockwork mouse.

"Nor me," said the sailor.

"Never mind," said the rabbit.

"What will happen to us now?" asked the mouse nervously.

The rabbit and the sailor knew they would probably be thrown away.

"Look at us," said the mouse sadly. "We're old and broken. Who would want to save us?"

"We might as well give up," agreed the sailor.

The rabbit nodded sadly. All three of them felt very glum.

The rabbit sat down by a wall by some cans of paint and packets of wallpaper paste. He looked down and noticed he was sitting on a small wooden box. It was covered in dust. The rabbit brushed it with his sleeve.

"Look at this!" he cried.

"What is it?" asked the mouse, coming over to see.

The sailor quickly helped the rabbit to lift the other things off the wooden box. When they rubbed more of the lid they could see that a lovely pattern covered the box.

"What's inside?" asked the mouse.

"I can't guess," said the sailor. "Let's open it and see."

Together they opened the lid. They looked inside. The mouse suddenly jumped back with a cry.

"Who's that?" she asked.

The others looked where the mouse was pointing. Sure enough there was a mouse, a sailor and a rabbit standing on the other side of the box looking back at them.

"Don't we know them?" asked the sailor.

"Why, it's us!" said the rabbit. "It's a mirror. We're looking at ourselves."

They all laughed. Then the mouse looked down into the box. "I know what this is," she said. "It's a jewellery box. Ladies keep rings and necklaces and earrings and jewels in them."

The rabbit climbed in to have a look. "There's someone in here," he said.

It was a figure of a dancer. She was a tiny ballerina.

"Of course!" said the mouse, who knew all about these things. "It's a musical jewellery box. My mistress used to have one. When you open the lid music plays and the ballerina dances."

The rabbit felt the little dancer move. "Hello," he said. "Are you all right?"

"Where am I?" asked the little dancer. "It was so dark for so long."

"Are you a dancer?" asked the sailor.

The little dancer looked sad. "A long time ago I was a dancer," she said. "The box was full of the most beautiful jewels you could ever see. Madame was always going out to balls and parties. The music would play on and on. And I would dance forever."

She looked down, her big brown eyes wet with tears.

"What happened?" asked the sailor.

"For many years I was very, very happy," said the little dancer. "But Madame grew older and older, and then she didn't come any more. The box stayed closed. There was no music. I didn't dance."

"What happened next?" asked the rabbit.

She went on, "After what seemed a long time someone opened the box. It was a man I'd never seen before. He took all the jewels away. Then he closed the box clumsily and broke me from my stand. Madame's things were all brought to this damp, dark place. When everything was sold I was left behind. I've been here ever since."

"You're still very beautiful," said the rabbit.

"I bet you can still dance beautifully too," said the sailor.

The little dancer shook her head. "No, I'm broken," she said. "Besides, nobody wants me any more. Just like you."

"Like us?" said the rabbit. He looked at the sailor and the mouse. "Why, we're going to fix ourselves up. We don't give up that easily, do we?"

"We don't?" asked the sailor.

"No, we don't!" said the mouse firmly.

"Here's paint and glue and tools and stuff," said the rabbit, pointing round the garage. "We'll mend ourselves."

"I'll repaint the sailor," said the mouse.

"And I'll take a look at your motor," said the sailor.

"You could glue on a new eye for me and mend my ear," said the rabbit to the little dancer. "And I can glue you back on your stand. What do you say?"

The little dancer thought carefully. "All right," she said. "We'll all help one another."

They all set to at once. Soon the sailor had a new coat of paint. The mouse's motor was mended. The rabbit had a new eye and a stitched ear. And the little dancer was back on her stand.

"Will you do a dance for us?" asked the rabbit.

The little dancer nodded. There was a silence. She didn't move. "I can't," she said. "I've forgotten how to dance."

No one knew what to do. The rabbit had never done a dance in his life. The sailor only knew how to dance the hornpipe. Then the mouse spoke up.

"Of course," she said. "This is a musical box. It must have music."

"There's no music in here," said the rabbit. "Just this old key."

"Aha," said the mouse. "Exactly what we need! You'll find a hole in the side of the box. Put the key inside and wind it up."

The music began to play. And the little dancer began to dance.

"I can dance!" she cried. "I can dance!"

And the four of them danced and danced the night away. Even the rabbit, who had never done a dance in his life. Then they fell asleep, tired out.

Early next morning the old man came to the garage. He looked through one or two of the boxes. Then he saw the old wooden music box. The rabbit, the sailor, the mouse and the dancer were all fast asleep in it.

"These look far too good to throw away," said the old man. "I'll save these for the next sale."

He took them inside the warm, dry house. He put them on the windowsill of his bedroom in the sunshine. He got used to seeing them when he woke up in the morning.

Often he would wind up the music box and watch the ballerina dance. And he would talk to the toys as if they were his friends.

When it came time for the next jumble sale he didn't want to part with them. Instead, he decided to buy them. They are still on his bedroom windowsill to this day.

And every time he plays the wooden music box it puts a little spring in his step. "Why," he says to the little dancer, laughing, "you make me feel like dancing. I'd forgotten how much fun it is!"

THE WEATHER

A SUNNY DAY

Today it is sunny. The weather is warm. The sun is shining. There are hardly any clouds in the sky. The sky is blue.

"I like it when it is a sunny day," says Bungle. "We can go out to play."

"I like it when it is dry and warm," says Zippy. "We can go for a swim."

"I like it when the sun shines," says George. "We can go for picnics. But I don't like it when it's too hot."

A RAINY DAY

Today it is raining. You cannot see the sun. The sky is full of dark clouds. They are full of rain.

"I don't like it when it's rainy," says Bungle. "We have to play indoors all the time."

"I like going for walks in the rain," says Zippy. "But I have to wear my raincoat and my wellington boots to keep dry. Do you like my umbrella?"

"The rain is good for the garden," says George. "It gives all the plants a drink."

A WINDY DAY

Today it is windy. The wind is blowing hard. All the clouds race across the sky. The wind blows things in the air.

"I don't mind when it's windy," says Zippy. "Then I can wear my favourite scarf. Look how it blows in the wind."

"When it's windy," says George, "I can fly my kite. Doesn't it fly high?"

A SNOWY DAY

Today it is snowing. All the ground is covered in white. The sky is very grey. The clouds are full of snow.

"I love it when it snows," says Bungle. "We can go in the garden and make a snowman."

"I like to ride on my sledge when it snows," says Zippy. "It goes very fast."

"I like to catch snowflakes," says George. "I catch them in my hand as they fall. They are such pretty patterns. I watch them melt in my hand."

33

MAKE YOUR OWN WEATHER CHART

Bungle, Zippy and George decide to make their own weather chart. Each day they look and see what the weather is like. Then they mark it on their chart. Would you like to make one too? Here's how to do it. Ask a grown up to help you.

You will need:

some cardboard
some paper
coloured pens, crayons or paints
cotton thread

sticky tape
drawing pins
non-toxic glue
round-ended scissors

MY WEATHER CHART
Today it is

1. Choose a big sheet of cardboard for your weather chart. You can colour it or paint a picture on it. Or maybe you can find a nice picture in a magazine to stick on it.
Label it MY WEATHER CHART
Near the top write in big letters: Today it is.

2. Stick a sheet of paper on some card. Divide it into strips. Write down all the different words for your weather chart like this:

Monday	sunny	rainy	windy
Tuesday	snowy	cloudy	foggy
Wednesday	wet	dry	cold
Thursday	warm	hot	frosty
Friday			
Saturday			
Sunday			

Stick another sheet of paper on some card. This time divide it into boxes. In the boxes draw some pictures to show what the weather is.

Cut up the strips and boxes. Cut some lengths of cotton. Stick these to the back of your strips and boxes with sticky tape.

Mount your weather chart on a board. Put drawing pins in so that you can hang your strips and boxes from them.

6. Each day you look out of your window to see what the weather is. Then you hang the right strips and boxes on your weather chart.

Can you think of any other words about the weather you can put on your chart?

WHATEVER THE WEATHER

Zippy, George and Bungle are busy in the garden. Geoffrey comes out to see what they are doing.

"You look busy," says Geoffrey.

"We are," says George. "We're working very hard."

"So I see," says Geoffrey. "What are you doing?"

"We're making a weather station, Geoffrey," says Zippy. "Do you like it?"

"It looks very good," says Geoffrey. "What does it do?"

"It helps us to tell what the weather is," says Bungle. "Then we can put it on our weather chart."

"Show me," says Geoffrey.

Bungle, Zippy and George show Geoffrey what they are making.

Bungle shows Geoffrey a

stick. He is making a flag to put on top.

"What does this do?" asks Geoffrey.

"It's to tell how strong the wind is," says Bungle.

George joins in. "It also tells us which way the wind is blowing. Look."

Bungle presses the stick into the ground. There is a breeze today. The breeze lifts the little flag. It flutters in the air.

"It's a little bit windy today," says George. "Look how it makes the flag fly."

"The wind is blowing this way," says Bungle. He shows Geoffrey which way the flag is blowing. "That means the wind is blowing from over there," he says.

"And what are you doing, Zippy?" asks Geoffrey. "That looks very interesting."

Zippy has put a jam jar on the ground. "This is my rain collector," says Zippy. "I put it on the ground. When the rain falls it goes inside. Each day I can come and look. It tells me how much rain we have."

"That's very clever," says Geoffrey. Geoffrey thinks the ideas are all very good.

Next day it is raining. The wind is blowing. The sky is full of dark clouds. George, Zippy and Bungle ask Geoffrey if they can go outside. They want to check their weather station.

Geoffrey thinks about it. "Only for a minute," says Geoffrey. "You must all put on your raincoats and wellington boots."

"And I can take my umbrella," says Zippy. "It will keep us dry."

They put on their things and go outside. Zippy looks in the jar. It has rainwater in. "Look in the jar," he says. "It's raining."

"I know," says George. "My coat is getting wet."

Bungle looks at the flag. It is blowing in the wind. "The wind is blowing hard," he says.

"I know," says Zippy. "The wind is blowing my umbrella inside out!"

Suddenly, the wind blows Zippy's umbrella out of his hand. It knocks over the jar, spilling all the water. Then it knocks over the flag.

"Oh no!" they cry.

"Time to come in," says Geoffrey, standing in the doorway.

Zippy, George and Bungle go inside. Their coats are wet. Zippy's umbrella is turned inside out.

"How is the weather station?" asks Geoffrey.

"We have a new weather station now," says Bungle.

"What's that?" asks Geoffrey.

"My coat is wet," says George, "so it must be raining!"

"And my umbrella is inside out," says Zippy, "so it must be windy!"

Then they dry off and warm themselves in front of the fire. Soon the sun is shining again and the sky is blue.

"Well," says Bungle, "there's an awful lot of weather today, isn't there, Geoffrey?"

And they all laugh.

THE TORTOISE RACE

Bungle, Zippy and George have found an exciting game to play. It is a race. But it is a funny kind of race because it's so slow. A tortoise goes very slowly, so they call the game The Tortoise Race. You can play too. Ask a grown up to help you

You need:
some card
three long pieces of string
round-ended scissors
three pencils
coloured pens or paints

Here's what you do:
1. Draw three tortoise shapes (like the one here) on a piece of card.
2. Cut them out.
3. Colour each one a different colour or pattern.
4. Make a hole in each one. Then thread a piece of string through and tie a knot.
5. Tie the other end of the string to a pencil.
6. Do this for each tortoise. Now you are ready to play. Put your tortoises in a line. Stretch out your string. When you shout, "Go!" wind your string round the pencil as fast as you can.

TWO BY TWO

All the animals have come to Noah to go on his big boat, the Ark. There are two of every animal. A pair of every animal. Noah is counting the pairs.

It is starting to rain and there is a loud clap of thunder. The animals are frightened. They run about all over the place.

Now they are all mixed up. Can you help? See if you can find the animals that go together. There are ten pairs of animals to find.

CHRISTMAS CUSTOMS

Christmas Cards

I'm dressed in Victorian clothes from a hundred years ago. I'm posting one of the first Christmas cards. It only costs a penny to post.

Today there are all sorts of Christmas cards. We like to make our own. We cut out pictures and stick them on card. Sometimes we draw our own.

Christmas Trees

I'm dressed as a Roman soldier from thousands of years ago. The Romans like to decorate trees at Christmas time too. We like to help Geoffrey dress the tree. Doesn't it look pretty with all its lights and decorations?

We use fir trees which have leaves all the year round. We call their leaves needles, because they are long and thin and sharp like needles.

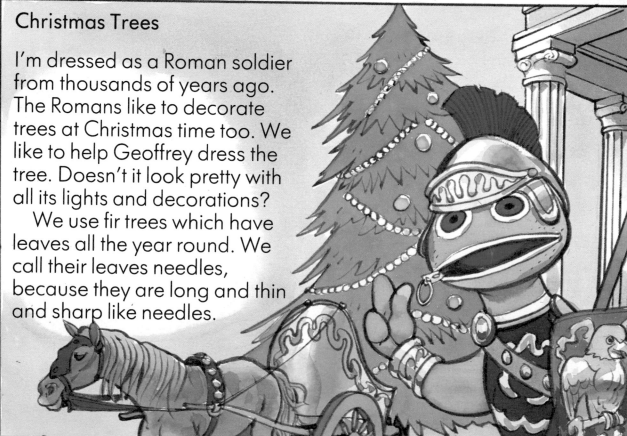

Holly

I'm dressed like an Ancient Briton from thousands of years ago. The holly grows its red berries especially for Christmas. They say it's lucky to bring some holly into the house on Christmas Eve.

The birds like the berries to eat, so they have their Christmas dinner too! Holly has very sharp leaves.

Santa Claus

I'm dressed like Santa Claus. He comes from the North Pole. The elves are busy all year round helping to make toys for girls and boys. Santa Claus flies through the air on a sleigh pulled by reindeer. He lands on your roof and comes down the chimney when you're asleep.

Be sure to leave Santa something to eat and drink. And don't forget something for the reindeer!

THE CHRISTMAS TREE

It is almost Christmas. Outside it is cold and windy. Bungle, Zippy and George are indoors in the warm. They are busy writing Christmas cards to their friends. They look at the pictures on the cards and choose which one they want to send to which friend.

"Here's one with lots of snow," says George, showing it to Bungle and Zippy. It has a picture of some boys and girls building a snowman.

"Here's one with people skating," says Bungle, showing his. Bungle's card has a picture of some people skating on ice.

"And I've found one with a sleigh," says Zippy, holding his card up. On Zippy's card there is a picture of a sleigh riding through the snow.

Geoffrey comes into the room. "It's lovely and warm in here," he says. He sees they are busy choosing their Christmas cards. Bungle, Zippy and

George show him which ones they like. Geoffrey looks at them carefully. He lays all three cards down side by side. "It looks very cold in all these pictures," he says.

Bungle, Zippy and George look at them. George shivers. "Brrrrr," he says. "It makes me feel cold looking at all that snow and ice."

"Yes," laughs Geoffrey. "Me too. It's good to be here in the warm. It's very, very cold outside at the moment."

"Is it snowing?" asks Bungle.

"No," says Geoffrey. "It doesn't always snow when it's cold, Bungle."

"Why is it so cold, Geoffrey?" asks George.

"Listen," says Geoffrey.

They are all quiet while they listen. They can hear the wind outside. "Woooooo," it goes, "wooooooo." The wind is blowing hard.

"The wind is making it so cold today," says Geoffrey.

They tell Geoffrey they are almost finished choosing their Christmas cards. Geoffrey is pleased. "The next thing we have to do is put up the Christmas decorations."

Geoffrey tries to remember exactly where the Christmas decorations are. Every year when the decorations are taken down after Christmas Geoffrey

They take the box of decorations into the living room. Geoffrey opens it. He begins to take out the things in the box one by one. There are paper streamers made in lots of different colours. There are big paper balls that hang from the ceiling. There are silver bells that hang from the wall or in the window. There are all sorts of things in the box.

They decide between them where everything should go. Zippy, George and Bungle choose the streamers and hand them to Geoffrey for him to hang up. When Zippy, George and Bungle look up they can see that Geoffrey is making a colourful pattern with them.

Then they choose where to hang the big paper balls and the bells. They save some things to put in other rooms in the house. Soon the whole house is beginning to feel full of Christmas cheer. They sit down for a rest.

"There are still some things missing," says Geoffrey.

"I know," says Zippy. "We don't have any mistletoe."

"And we don't have any holly," says Bungle.

"We need a Christmas tree as well," adds George. "Look. There are all these decorations

puts them away safely until the next Christmas. He looks on top of the wardrobe. He looks in the attic. Then he remembers. The Christmas decorations are in a box in the cupboard under the stairs.

Bungle, Zippy, George and Geoffrey go and look for the box. They have to take one or two things out of the cupboard first.

"Ah, here it is," says Geoffrey at last. He brings out a cardboard box with the words 'Christmas decorations' written on the side. Geoffrey puts the other things away.

to put on the tree."

Geoffrey smiles. "I have a surprise," he says. He goes out of the room. He comes back a few moments later, carrying a shopping bag. Inside is some holly, and a small branch of mistletoe. George, Bungle and Zippy decide where to put them and Geoffrey hangs them up.

"Have you got a Christmas tree as well, Geoffrey?" asks George.

"Not yet," says Geoffrey. "I thought we could go and choose one tomorrow. Is there anything else in the box?"

Bungle has a look. "Just this coloured string and lots of little coloured things. What are they for?"

"I remember," says Zippy. "We hang the Christmas cards we receive on the string. The little coloured things are pegs to hold them on."

They put the cards on to the coloured string with the pegs. Then Geoffrey hangs the strings of cards from the wall. They all stand back to admire their work.

Geoffrey looks at his watch. "Nearly time for bed," he says.

"Can we finish writing our cards first?" asks Bungle.

"Yes, all right," replies Geoffrey.

They look for the cards. They cannot find them. "Where can they have gone?" asks Zippy.

George laughs out loud. "I know," he says. He points to the strings of Christmas cards hanging from the walls. "We've hung them up with the others by mistake."

They all laugh together. Then they try and remember which ones are the ones they are sending, and which are the ones other people have sent to them. After a little while it is all sorted out. They finish writing their cards and put them in envelopes ready to deliver.

All that is needed now is a Christmas tree and the house is decorated ready for Christmas. As they go to bed they can still

hear the sound of the wind outside. "Wooowooo," it goes, "wooowooo."

In the morning when they wake up it is still quite cold, but it is quiet outside. The wind is not blowing any more. They sit down to breakfast.

"After breakfast," says Geoffrey, "we can go and buy a Christmas tree. And we need to find a tub or a bucket to put it in."

George is thoughtful. "Where do Christmas trees come from, Geoffrey?" he asks.

"They grow in the ground," Geoffrey replies. "People like farmers grow them. There are trees for sale in the shop down the road."

George carries on eating his

breakfast, but he has a puzzled look on his face. Before they get ready to go out and buy the Christmas tree, George has one more question to ask.

"Geoffrey, do the farmers have to cut the trees down or dig them up?" he asks.

"Some of them are cut down," says Geoffrey. "Others are dug up. If they have roots on you can sometimes plant them again after Christmas. You have to throw the others away because they can't grow again."

George isn't happy about this. "If I was a tree," he says, "I don't think I'd like to be dug up or cut down, would you?"

"But we have to have a Christmas tree, George," says Zippy, "or it isn't a proper Christmas!"

"What do you think, Bungle?" asks Geoffrey.

Bungle is not sure. "Now I think about it," he says, "George is right. I wouldn't like it if I was a tree. But Zippy is right as well. It isn't a proper Christmas without a tree. What can we do, Geoffrey?"

They all look at Geoffrey to see if he has the answer. He has a good, long think. While he is thinking he looks out of the window. Suddenly he says, "I

know just the thing. Look in the garden."

They all look out of the window. There on the lawn is part of a branch that has fallen from the tree at the bottom of the garden. The wind has blown it down during the night. Zippy, George, Bungle and Geoffrey all put their coats and shoes on and go to have a look.

Geoffrey explains his idea. "We put this branch upright in the tub, just like a real Christmas tree," he says. "But first we paint it white so it looks like it is covered with snow. Then we hang all the tree decorations from the little branches."

The others think this is a great idea. They set to work. With Geoffrey's help it is soon painted. When it is dry they put it in the tub and take it into the house. They put some Christmas wrapping paper round the tub. Then they all help to hang the decorations from the tree.

Soon it is all finished. They look round the room. There are streamers and silver bells, paper balls and Christmas cards, mistletoe and holly. Their home-made Christmas tree looks wonderful.

"All done," says Geoffrey. "Now all we have to do is wait for Father Christmas!"

BITS AND PIECES

"People throw away lots of things," says Bungle.

"But we know some really good things to do with bits and pieces people throw away," says George. "Don't we, Geoffrey?"

Geoffrey smiles and nods. Bungle, Zippy and George are very busy making things. "Always ask a grown up to help," says Geoffrey.

I use old corks to make a fishing game. Geoffrey helps me. Geoffrey cuts a slit across the cork. Then he puts a screw in the bottom.

While he does that I draw a fish's head on a piece of card, just like this. I colour it on both sides.

Then Geoffrey finds a stick and ties on a piece of string. He puts a hook on the end. He makes a fishing rod.

We make a hole in the nose of the fish and slide the fish head into the cork. Now we fill a bowl with water. We put the fish in and try to hook it out. With more corks we can make more fish.

I use empty matchboxes. I ask Geoffrey for them. I collect ones that are the same size. With Geoffrey's help I stick the boxes together. It makes a little nest of drawers.

Geoffrey sticks the boxes to a strong piece of cardboard. Now I paint the boxes all sorts of colours.

Geoffrey puts little paper fasteners in each drawer to make handles. I use the drawers to keep all my special shells and stones in.

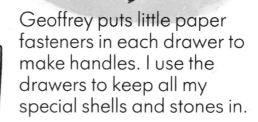

I use old cornflake boxes. I make twizzers with them. Geoffrey cuts out a circle for me from the box. We choose part of the box with lots of colours on.

I paint some more colours on the other side. Geoffrey makes two holes in the middle. We thread a piece of string (50cm long) through the hole, then back through the other. Then Geoffrey joins one end of the string to the other.

Holding the twizzer like this I swing it over and over like this. When the string is all twisted round, I make the string tight or slack to spin the twizzer round. Watch the patterns change!

The leaves fall from the trees in the autumn. Our garden is full of them.

We collect the best ones. We put them between layers of tissue paper. Then we put them between some heavy books.

After a few days we take them out. We use them to make patterns with. Geoffrey helps us to stick the leaves on paper. We make lots of lovely leaf pictures.

"I'm collecting old stamps," says Bungle. "The local hospital sells them to buy toys for the children's ward."

"I'm collecting milk bottle tops," says Zippy. "It helps to make money for the school. The metal from the bottle tops can be used again."

"I'm collecting lots of old newspapers," says George. "It helps to make money for the community centre. The paper can be used again and not wasted."

THE LETTER

It is a bright, sunny morning. Bungle is the first out of bed. He washes and dresses. Then he goes downstairs.

At the bottom of the stairs Bungle stops. He looks down at the mat behind the front door. On it is the daily newspaper. It is Geoffrey's.

Bungle bends down to pick it up. As he does, he notices something underneath it. It is a letter. He takes it with the newspaper and puts it by Geoffrey's place at the breakfast table.

Zippy and George are soon downstairs too. Geoffrey walks in.

"Good morning," says Geoffrey. "You are all up early."

"Good morning, Geoffrey. You are up early too," say Zippy, George and Bungle.

"I put your newspaper and your letter ready for you on the table, Geoffrey," says Bungle.

They all eat their breakfasts. Then Geoffrey says, "I have a surprise for you."

"What is it?" asks Bungle.

"I like surprises," says George.

"Tell us, Geoffrey, please," says Zippy.

"It's this letter," says Geoffrey.

"Who is it from?" asks Bungle.

"I don't know," says Geoffrey.

"Don't be silly, Geoffrey," says Zippy. "You must know!"

"But the letter isn't open yet," says Geoffrey.

"Why not, Geoffrey?" asks Bungle.

"That's the surprise," says Geoffrey. He hands the letter to Bungle. "Look at it, Bungle. What does it say on the envelope?"

Bungle takes the letter. He reads the envelope slowly. He reads it again.

"What does it say, Bungle?" asks George, trying to see.

"Give it to me," says Zippy. "I can read it. I'm a good reader."

Bungle doesn't need to give it to Zippy. "It says *Bungle* on the envelope," says Bungle. "What does that mean, Geoffrey?"

"It means that the letter is for you, Bungle," laughs Geoffrey.

"Why does someone want to write to me?" asks Bungle.

"We can't find out what the letter says until you open it," says Zippy.

"And we can't find out who it is from," says George.

"Yes, come on, Bungle!" says Geoffrey. "Open the letter."

"Yes, come on, Bungle!" say Zippy and George.

Bungle opens the letter carefully. He takes care not to tear it. Inside is a sheet of writing paper. Bungle reads it.

"It's from a friend," says Bungle, "from our holiday by the seaside. The nice lady from the guest house."

"May we hear it?" asks Geoffrey.

Bungle clears his throat. He puts on his best reading voice.

"*Dear Bungle, it says.*"

"That's you," says George.

Zippy tells George to be quiet and listen.

Bungle goes on, "*I am glad you like our little seaside town. You are always welcome to come and stay with me. I hope Zippy, George and Geoffrey are well.*"

"That's me!" says Zippy.

"And me!" says George.

"And Geoffrey too," adds Bungle.

"How does it end, Bungle?" asks Geoffrey.

"It says, *I hope to see you again soon. Lots of love, Mrs Adams,*" says Bungle.

"Isn't that nice of her?" says Geoffrey. "You must write and thank her right away, Bungle."

"How?" asks Bungle.

"Write a letter back," says Geoffrey.

"But I don't know how to write a letter," says Bungle. "I don't know what to say."

"I'll help you," says Geoffrey.

"So will we!" say George and Zippy.

Everyone helps to wash and

dry the breakfast things. Then they are ready to start.

"First we need a pen and paper," says Geoffrey. "Zippy, there is a pen by the telephone. George, there is some writing paper on my desk."

Zippy and George bring the pen and paper. "This paper already has writing on, George," says Geoffrey. "It must be clean paper for a letter."

George fetches some clean paper. Bungle is ready to begin. "What do I write first?" asks Bungle.

"First, you must put your address," says Geoffrey.

"What is an address, Geoffrey?" asks George.

"It's where you live," says Geoffrey. "First, the name or number of your house. Then, the name of the road we live on. Next comes the village or town. Last of all is the post code."

"What's a coast pode, Geoffrey?" asks Zippy.

"Not coast pode, Zippy — post code. Each road has its own special code," says Geoffrey. "A code is a mixture of letters and numbers. It helps the postman deliver the letter more quickly."

Soon Bungle has his address written down.

"What next, Geoffrey?" asks Bungle.

"Next comes the date," says Geoffrey. "Look on the calendar, George."

George looks at the calendar on the wall. He tells Bungle the day, the month, and the year. Bungle writes it down.

"I know what comes next," says Zippy. "It's *Dear Mrs Adams.*"

"That's quite right," says Geoffrey.

"Now we have to decide what to say to her," says

Bungle. "I know. We can tell her about the rest of our holiday, after the seaside."

The letter is nearly finished. "I know what comes at the end," says George. "You have to put *With lots of love from Bungle.*"

Bungle does. "The letter is ready now," he says. He puts it in an envelope and seals it up.

"There are still three more things to do," says Geoffrey. "Can you guess what they are?"

George, Zippy and Bungle think hard. "I know!" says George. "We have to write Mrs Adams' address on the envelope. Otherwise the postman won't know where to take it."

"Oh dear," says Bungle. "I don't know what her address is."

"Yes you do, Bungle," says Geoffrey. "Look at her letter."

Bungle does. Mrs Adams has put her address at the top – just like Bungle has on his letter.

"I think I know what the second thing is," says Zippy. "We have to put a stamp on."

"That's right, Zippy," says Geoffrey. "I have one in my wallet."

Bungle licks the stamp and sticks it on. "One more thing to do," says Bungle. "I wonder what it can be?"

Bungle, George and Zippy think very hard. At last Bungle gives a great big smile. "I know, Geoffrey," he says. "We have to post it!"

"Yes," says Geoffrey. "Let's all walk down to the postbox."

CARDS AND LETTERS

"We like to make our own cards," says Bungle.

"We can write letters on them," says Zippy.

"Or we can use them as birthday cards," says George.

Here is what you need:
card or paper
non-toxic glue
round-ended scissors
old magazines, seed catalogues and Christmas cards
envelopes to fit

"Or as Christmas cards," says Bungle.

"Or postcards," says Zippy.

"Even as invitation cards for a party," says George.

Geoffrey helps George, Bungle and Zippy. He finds some paper or card to make the cards with. He cuts it to the right size to fit the envelopes.

"I ask Geoffrey for some old magazines," says Bungle. "There are pictures of cars and aeroplanes and boats. Geoffrey cuts them out and I stick them on the front of the card."

"I ask Geoffrey for old seed catalogues," says George. "They are full of pictures of flowers and trees. There are all sorts of colours and shapes. Geoffrey cuts them out and I stick them on the front of the card."

"I ask Geoffrey for the old Christmas cards," says Zippy. "You can find all kinds of good pictures on them. Some are best for making new Christmas cards. Others you can use for any cards. Geoffrey cuts them out and I stick them on the front of the cards."

"Here's one of my cards," says Bungle. "Here is a blue racing car."

"Here's one of my cards," says George. "Here are some red roses."

"And here's one of my cards," says Zippy. "Here are two rabbits with white tails."

THE LETTER GAME

The aim of the game is to be the first one to write and post a letter. On the coloured squares are the things you need to write or post your letter: paper (RED), a pen (BLUE), an envelope (GREEN), and a stamp (YELLOW). Choose if you want to play Zippy, George, Bungle or Geoffrey. Place your big counter on that starting place. You each need four other small counters. Throw the dice and move only in straight lines. You can move across or down the board, or diagonally. You can change direction at the start of each move.

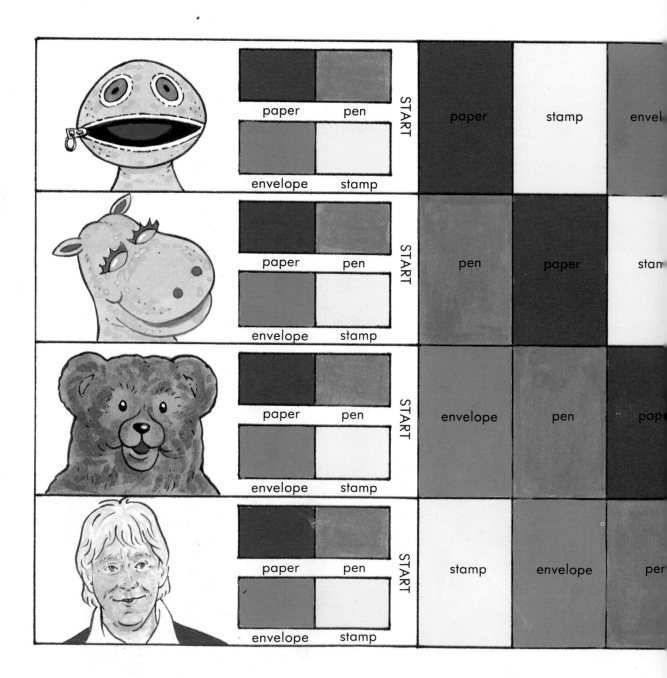